My 100 Hands Go To School

by Lauryn Marie Burks

Illustrations by Giovanna Adams

www.My100Hands.com

My 100 Hands Go To School
by Lauryn Marie Burks
www.My100Hands.com

Illustrations by Giovanna Adams
www.polka-dot-illustrations.com

Copyright © 2014 Munchkin Power, LLC

All rights reserved. Except as permitted under U.S. Copyright Act of 1976, no part of this publication may be reproduced, distributed, or transmitted in any form or by any means, or stored in a database or retrieval system, without the prior written permission of the publisher.

Published by Munchkin Power, LLC
6338 Snider Rd, Suite 274
Mason, OH 45040
www.munchkinpowerllc.com

ISBN: 978-0-9883252-5-8
Printed in the United States of America

The alarm was ringing at 7 o'clock. My 100 Hands were saying, "Come on Lauryn! Come on Lauryn! Get up! Get up! It's the first day of school for us. We're so excited! Get up! Get up!" "Alright, alright. I'm getting up", I said.

1

"Let's do our exercises", said the Healthy Hand Twins, Sporty and Sportette. We stretched. We ran in place and did jumping jacks.

2

After we exercised, we brushed our teeth, washed our faces and put on our clothes.

Next, My 100 Hands cooked breakfast. We had bacon, waffles, and milk.

At 8 o'clock, My 100 Hands walked me to the bus stop. When the bus driver saw the hands, she said, "Oh my goodness! Where did you get all of these hands?" "It's a long story", I said.

I was going to sit next to my friend Tristen, but My 100 Hands wanted to sit all the way in the back of the bus.

6

Some of the kids were not getting along on the bus. They were not paying attention, while the hands were introducing themselves. That made me sad.

When we got off the bus, Helpful Hand and I talked to the kids. We told them that their behavior was not good. They said they were sorry.

When we got to school, the kids in my class screamed. They were so surprised that I brought My 100 Hands to school.

Some kids ran behind the Teacher. Some kids had funny looks on their faces. I said, "Everything is OK. My 100 Hands are nice. They would like to play with you."

My 100 Hands like gym, art, music, and library, just like me. Smarty Hand likes reading too.

When he got to the library, he was so excited. He zoomed around the library, reading all of the books!

Helpful Hand likes science.

Pretty Hand likes art. She likes being creative.

Safety Hand likes gym.

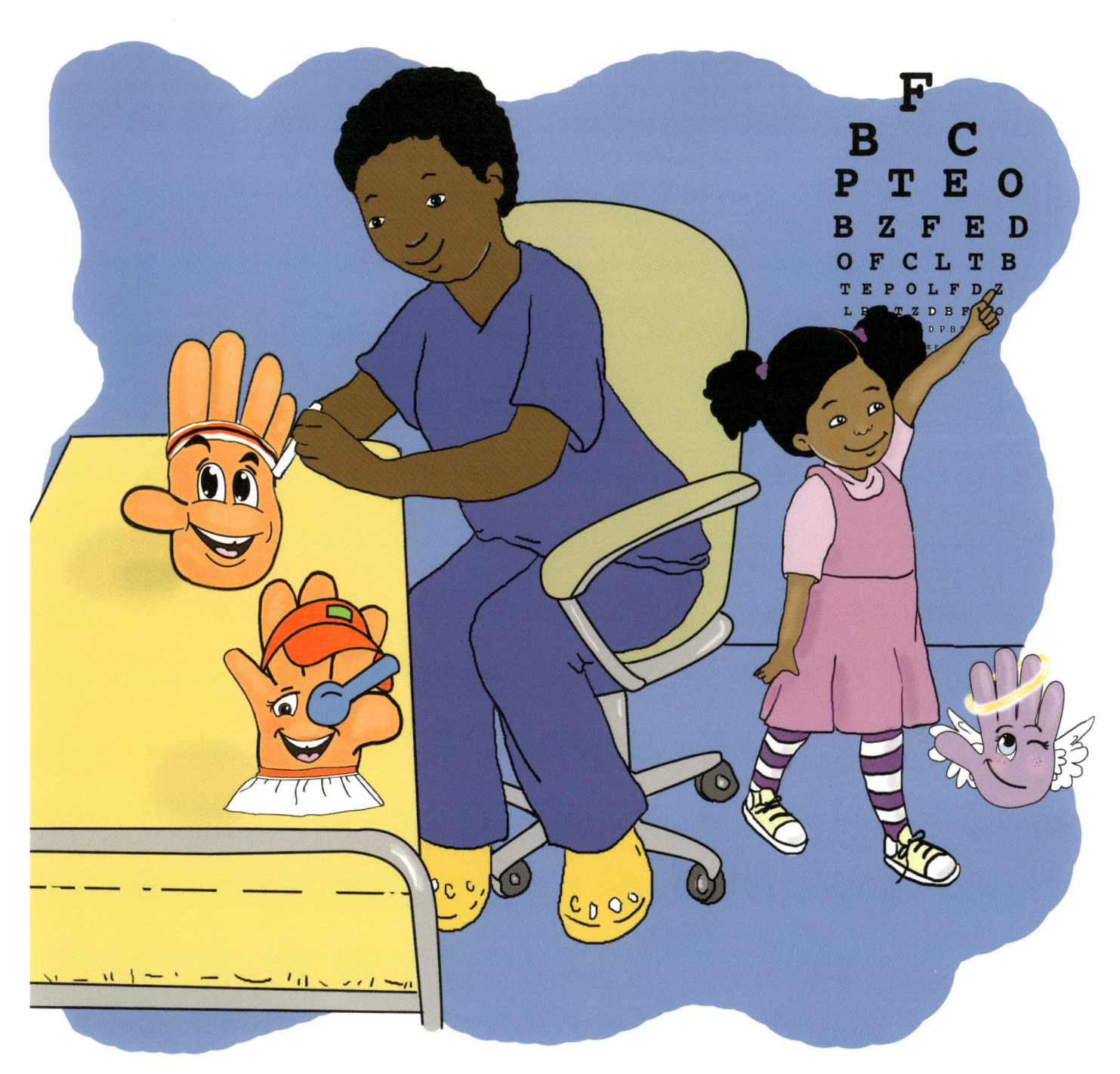

The Healthy Hand Twins, Sporty and Sportette, like going to see the nurse and getting their eyes checked.

My 100 Hands like lunch too. They like to eat fruits, veggies, and all kinds of healthy stuff.

17

Some of the kids tried to get the hands to eat candy. I talked to the kids and told them that they don't like to eat candy.

When the bell rang, it was time for recess. My 100 Hands went outside to play with my friends. Everyone was screaming and having fun.

Happy Hand changed into his swim suit. He turned on the water hose and made the slide into a waterslide. All the kids were so amazed! They changed into their swimsuits and went down the slide too.

The Teacher was not happy with Happy Hand, because today was not water play day.

21.

Happy Hand was sent to the Principal's office.

Happy Hand was sad. So, he went to apologize to the Teacher.

23

After school, My 100 Hands wanted to cheer Happy Hand up by singing a silly song. They sang the birthday song, even though it was not his birthday! Happy Hand felt better.

24

25

When we got home from school, everyone did their homework.

At dinner time, My 100 Hands made a big mess. Some spilled their drinks and food.

Helpful Hand reminded My 100 Hands to always clean up after themselves.

28

After dinner, My 100 Hands were filthy. So, they took a bath.

30

At bedtime, Thankful Hand said a prayer for everyone.

My 100 Hands fell fast asleep.

All went to sleep except Happy Hand. He kept getting out of bed. I hope he does not get into any more trouble.

The End

Meet The 100 Hands™

Helpful Hand

Helpful Hand™ – He provides assistance by teaching manners, sharing, being friendly, cooperating, and building lasting relationships.

Happy Hand

Happy Hand™ – He teaches everyone to be content, blissful, in high spirits, have a positive attitude, and to remember the glass is always half full.

Pretty Hand

Pretty Hand™– She helps develop self-awareness, self-confidence, charisma, and integrity.

Safety Hand

Safety Hand™– He promotes well being, security, and protecting yourself from accidents and harmful situations.

Sporty

Sporty™ – He is the healthiest hand. He encourages everyone to eat right, get exercise, and be a good sport.

Healthy Hand Twins

Healthy Hand Twins™ – They teach all to be aware of their physical and mental health.

Sportette

Sportette™ – She teaches everyone to give their best effort everytime. A fierce competitor, even the boys want her on their team.

Thankful Hand

Thankful Hand™ – She teaches everyone about gratitude and the importance of having a spiritual connection to the universe and others around them.

Smarty Hand

Smarty Hand™ – He encourages everyone to be diligent in their schoolwork and make good decisions.

Create-A-Hand

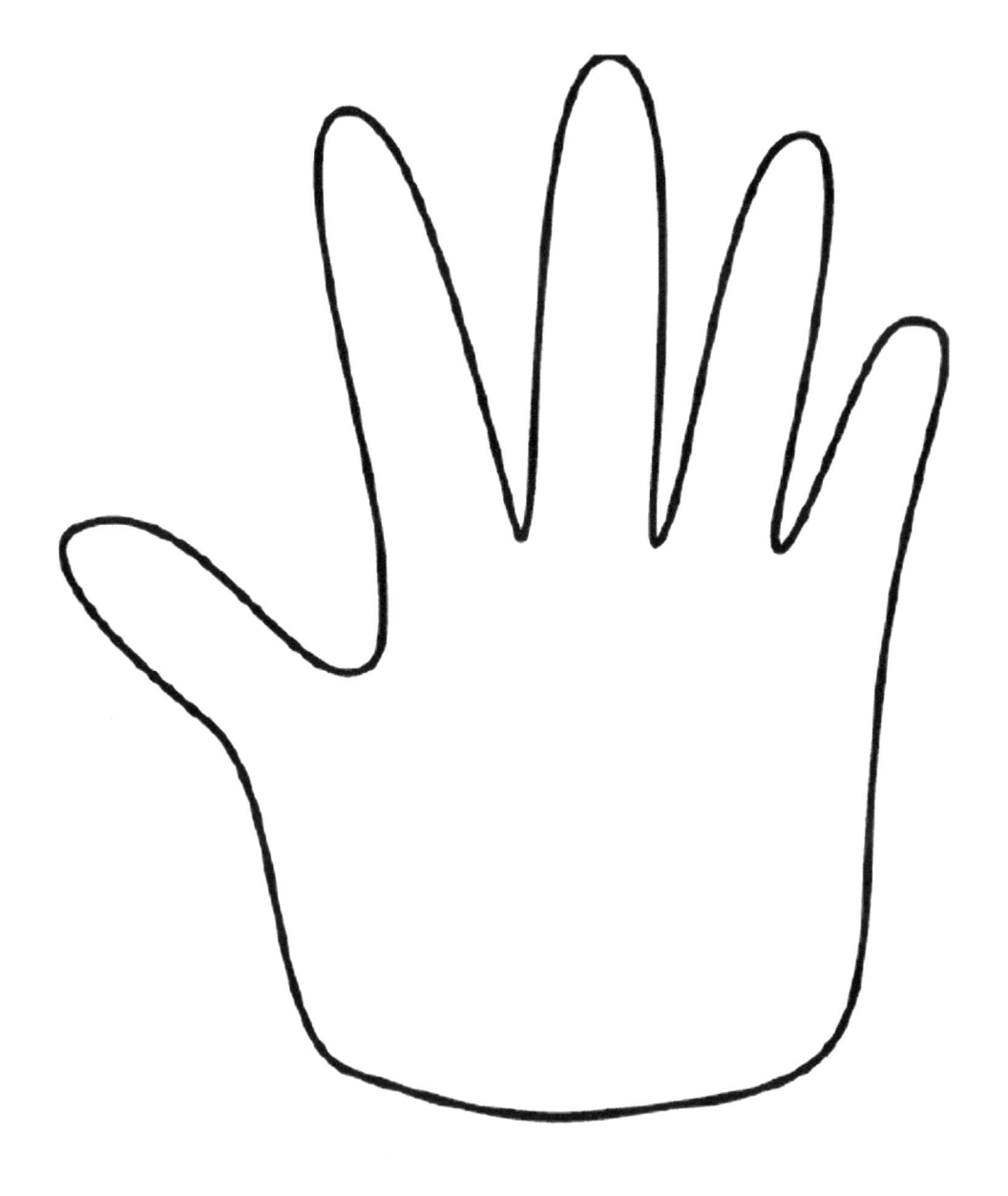

Use this space to create a new hand

Create-A-Hand

Use this space to create a new hand

About the Author

Lauryn Marie Burks is a bright, articulate, imaginative child. She loves participating in Children's Church, reading books, singing songs, dancing and watching her favorite movies. An aspiring actress, she is not shy about making new experiences, and she is warm and friendly to everyone she meets.

Lauryn Marie Burks

The first story, My 100 Hands, was created by Lauryn when she was just 5 years old. While faced with the constant challenge of staying on task and dealing with hurried parents, Lauryn day-dreamed about having 100 little friendly hands that would help her perform various tasks and chores. Seeing the first book come to life, she immediately started creating the second story of the series, My 100 Hands Go To School.

Munchkin Power

Harness the creative energy and ideas of your kid! Visit our website and share your kid's amazing accomplishments.

www.munchkinpowerllc.com

CPSIA information can be obtained at www.ICGtesting.com
Printed in the USA
BVIW12n1218100515
399555BV00002B/3